To Dad, with love and thanks for coming to
watch me every time I've tried to be a dancer!
Manny

ALADDIN PAPERBACKS
An imprint of Simon & Schuster Children's Publishing Division
1230 Avenue of the Americas, New York, NY 10020
Copyright © 2001 by Mandy Stanley
First published in Great Britain in 2001 by HarperCollins Publishers Ltd.
First U.S. edition 2002
All rights reserved, including the right of reproduction in whole or in part in any form.
ALADDIN PAPERBACKS and colophon are registered trademarks of Simon & Schuster, Inc.
Also available in a Simon & Schuster Books for Young Readers hardcover edition.
Designed by Molly Dallas
The text of this book was set in Bernhard Gothic.
Manufactured in China
First Aladdin Paperbacks edition February 2005
4   6   8   10   9   7   5   3
Library of Congress Control Number 2001088917
ISBN 0-689-84797-1 (hc.)
ISBN 0-689-87608-4 (Aladdin pbk.)

Lettice

The Dancing Rabbit
Mandy Stanley

ALADDIN PAPERBACKS

New York , London   Toronto   Sydney

Lettice Rabbit and her family lived high up on the top of the hill. Nibble, nibble, hop, hop. Every day was the same . . .

until the day Lettice saw a picture pinned to a tree. It was then she knew that she wanted to be a dancer more than anything else in the world.

Lettice hopped to Town all by herself. She'd never been so far from home in her life.

It was exciting. There were lots of busy people, noisy babies, chatty children, and great big dogs!

Lettice peeped in an open door—and saw
dancers just like in the picture.

"Please may I join in?" asked Lettice shyly.

"Yes," said the surprised teacher, "but first
you must get dressed in ballet clothes."

Lettice didn't know what to do—she had never worn clothes before.

"You can get them at the shop where we get ours," called out a little girl.

At the shop Lettice tried on all the clothes,

but the dress dragged
on the floor,

the shoes were
like flippers,

and the sweater
was huge.

Lettice began
to cry.

Then the clerk brought out
a ballerina doll.

All the doll's clothes
fit perfectly.

Now Lettice was ready!

Lettice hopped back to the ballet class.
First, she had to learn the ballet positions.
She watched and listened very carefully.
The ballet teacher showed her how to hold
her head high so her ears would look
graceful.

Lettice worked very
hard. She turned out
her long toes,

she stretched up her arms,

and she tried not to wobble.

When she jumped . . .

it looked as though she were flying! When she

twirled and whirled, she was almost a blur.

Every week, Lettice went to Town for her class, and at home she practiced every spare minute of the day.

The teacher thought Lettice was very special and was amazed at her extraordinary jumps.

Lettice worked so hard that each night she went to bed very tired—but happy.

A few weeks later it was time for the
end-of-term show. Lettice had been chosen
for the starring role. She had a gorgeous
costume—there was even a tiny crown!

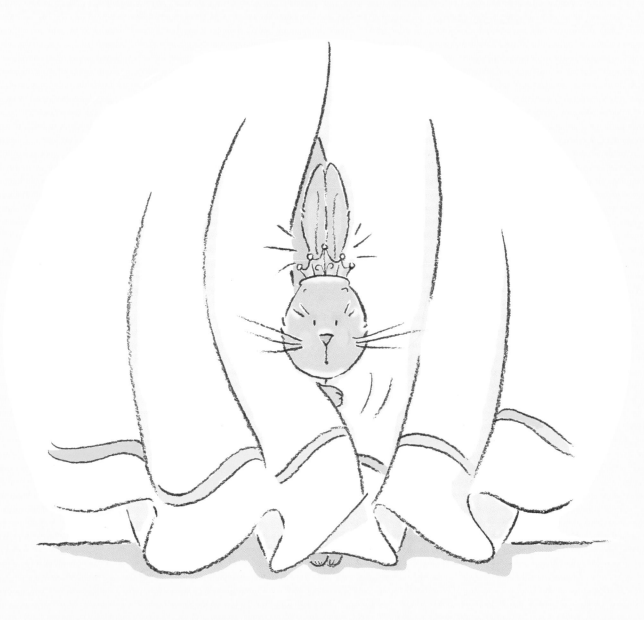

All of Lettice's family had come to see her.
Lettice was so nervous she thought she
wouldn't be able to dance at all!

The lights went down, and the music began. Lettice took a deep breath . . . and leaped onto the stage.

She glittered and twinkled and soared through the air.

The Rabbit family was so proud, they clapped their soft little paws all through the show.

When it was all over, Lettice and the other dancers were talking about the fun they had had. The Rabbit family didn't want to bother her, so they went home.

"Wait for me," squeaked Lettice, but they didn't hear her.

Poor Lettice was tired and alone. As she slowly walked home, it began to rain. She just wanted to crawl into the warm, cozy burrow and fall fast asleep.

The next day the Rabbit family was busy collecting apples, cabbages, and carrots for a picnic.

"Lettice won't want to come," said her brothers and sisters. "She's a star now!"

Lettice felt very hurt. How could they go without her?

She pulled off the crown and threw off the dress. She kicked off her shoes and scrambled out of her tights.

"Wait for me!" she cried, racing up the hill.
She could feel the sun on her fur, the grass
between her toes, and the wind in her ears.
It was wonderful!

Lettice had found out what it felt like
to be a ballerina, but she knew that being
a rabbit was, by far, the very best thing
in the world.